PARVATHY'S WELL & OTHER STORIES

POORNIMA MANCO

In memory of my mother.

"The world is but a canvas to our imagination"
Henry David Thoreau

If you'd like a FREE story, sign up at www.poornimamanco.com/free!

CONTENTS

PARVATHY'S WELL

SHE LOVED STARING into the well those long, lazy summer afternoons. The sticky heat, the low buzzing of the flies, the trees that swayed in the occasional breeze, would all lull her into a strange stupor. She'd throw little stones into the well and watch the concentric ripples with a mild fascination. Her imagination would make up little stories about fantastical creatures that lived under the water. She'd wonder if they were watching her, just as she was watching them... a thin veil of water separating the two worlds. Perhaps, some were quite amiable; wanting to be friends, to laugh and play with her... or perhaps they were monstrous beasts - hungry, salivating, waiting for one misstep to swallow her whole. She'd laugh at her fancies, and chuck a load of pebbles, watching the splashes with delight. At nine, life was a comforting routine of school, a home with *Amma*[1] and *Appa*[2], two brothers, and her vast garden overgrown with dense foliage, hidden amongst which was her special, mysterious well.

It had become almost routine to spend her afternoons by its side. Appa would be at work. Her brothers worked in the city. Amma would give her a light lunch of *rasam*[3] and rice, and then pat her on the head absently and say, "Go and play, *molé*[4]." Obligingly, Parvathy would take her miniature wooden truck and the doll with the missing arm into the garden and while away those afternoons daydreaming. Speculating about the world that lay beneath that cool, still water. A magical world where anything was possible.

She was a shy girl of few words. A late, surprise entrant into the world, she seemed almost to apologise for her existence. After all, *Amma* and *Appa*'s family had been complete till she decided to appear. Her brothers had been in their late teens and profoundly embarrassed. Her father had viewed her as an inconvenience. Only *Amma* seemed to want her... and then not.

Parvathy curled a tendril of her hair around her finger. She could remember the hugs and the kisses. Being gently rocked to sleep. Yet, that too had faded over time. *Amma* was always busy. Trying to feed and care for three grown men seemed to leave her no time for the slight, anxious girl who always hovered in the shadows.

A ripple of laughter erupted from the house. Mohan uncle must have arrived. Like the well, the house and her family, he was another constant in her life. He came most weeks to deliver merchandise for *Appa*. Some days he came in the evening, and all the men would sit and drink hot sweetened cups of tea, and polish off plates of freshly fried *pakoras*.[5] Other days he'd come in the afternoons. He was well liked by the family. He was *Amma*'s distant cousin, on her father's side. Tall and broad shouldered with a big black moustache, he had the whitest smile Parvathy had ever seen. Even *Amma* seemed calmer, almost happier, in his presence.

She wanted to go in and mutter a shy hello as she had sometimes done. He always laughed and pulled her towards him. Then with a flourish he would produce a sweet out of his pocket and present it to her. *Amma* would smile at these exchanges and Parvathy would squirm with happiness. Of late, however, she could sense that *Amma* was not happy if she came in unannounced. Once *Amma* had said quite sternly, "*Molé*[6], I told you to play outside. You must not interrupt adult talk."

Parvathy never did again. She would often hear snippets of conversations inadvertently. Sometimes *Amma* would sigh, other times giggle. Once she looked like she'd been weeping. Mohan uncle reminded her of home... of her family, her brothers and sisters she'd had to leave behind at sixteen when she'd been married off to *Appa*. Parvathy was happy that at least *Amma* had not lost all contact with her family. The distance between the villages was so great that *Amma* hadn't been to see them in six years. She had to make do with the sporadic letters and the tidbits that Mohan uncle brought her.

A drum roll of thunder startled her out of her thoughts. Two fat drops of rain fell on her arm. She licked them off in excitement. It was the first of the rains heralding the arrival of the monsoon. The gentle drizzle turned into a heavy downpour within minutes. Parvathy snatched her doll and ran inside. She was soaked through. She grabbed a towel and started to dry her hair. Quickly she undressed and leaving the sodden pile on the floor pulled an old, faded dress off the peg. It was then that she heard it. The sound was something between a snort and a grunt.

She peered into the living room but there was no one to be seen. The merchandise lay on the floor abandoned. The clipboard and pen lay next to it, inventory half done. Two cups of barely drunk tea sat forlornly on the little side table.

In a panic, her eyes cast around for her mother. Where was *Amma*? Then she heard it again. That odd sound coming from her mother's room. The door was shut. She didn't dare open it for fear of finding some alien creature behind it. Instead, she carefully and quietly clambered on to the table propped next to the wall and peered in through the little mesh window.

Parvathy nearly screamed in horror. She had to clamp her hand over her mouth and steady herself. It looked like her mother was being assaulted by a boar. Her eyes were closed and her hair swanned around her head like a fan. Her *saree*[7] had been pushed up to her waist. The creature, whose back was covered in black fur, was holding her down and pushing, pushing into her. He grunted as he collapsed on her. Her mother opened her eyes and wept. Parvathy nearly seized the knife from the kitchen to go attack the beast.

Then the strangest thing happened. Her mother smiled and cradled the creature's face and kissed it. Her heart knocking wildly against her rib cage, Parvathy lowered herself hastily. She ran to the toilet and retched till there was nothing left but her heaving empty stomach. She stayed in her room all afternoon feigning a headache, her mind still reeling from the shocking image of her mother and that repugnant monster.

The next few days she watched her mother silently. Her shadowy presence was as insubstantial as ever but now there was a subversive purpose to her stalking. She was convinced her mother had been possessed by an evil entity. What else could explain that bizarre, horrific scene she had unwittingly witnessed?

She noticed now, how different *Amma* was in *Appa*'s presence. She was quiet and timid, a docile wife, barely speaking unless spoken to. Her brothers too treated her with a quiet condescension that she bore smilingly. Yet, in their absence, she was a different person. Always humming and laughing. Preening in front of the mirror. Oiling her thick, beautiful hair. Putting kohl in her doe-like eyes. Trying on different *sarees* till she found a favourite. Aligning the dot just right on her forehead.

She now shrank from her mother's touch, and withdrew even further from her. This was not her mother! Not the woman who had birthed her. How could it be? This was some sort of abomination. A parasite from the netherworld sucking all the love and goodness out of her birth mother.

Her mind was made up. Too scared to approach *Appa*, she put a letter in his shirt pocket before he left for work, detailing all that she had seen and heard.

That afternoon as she played with her doll, she heard an unearthly wailing emerging from the house. She ran in to be confronted with *Appa* yanking at *Amma*'s hair as she screamed in agony. Mohan uncle was hastily tidying up the merchandise, his shirt falling open to reveal his hairy chest. Her brothers stood by the door, shocked and uncomprehending.

For a brief instant, her mother's eyes met hers - anguished and pleading. Parvathy shuddered as *Amma* was dragged away.

It was a tense evening with little food and no conversation. Her stomach churned all night. She slept fitfully. Her dreams were strange and terrifying. She longed to crawl into bed with *Amma* and cling to her. At last, exhausted, she fell into a deep sleep.

She awoke late the next morning. The police were already there. The well had been sealed off. Parvathy's last glimpse of her precious well was of a doll with no arm floating placidly, entangled in a deep crimson *saree*.

LAJJO

6AM: The cacophony of the birds is louder this morning. One jarring squawk crashes into another, building into a tuneless crescendo. I try to fall back to sleep, to no avail. The room feels oppressive; the air stale. Spring is slowly giving way to Summer, and the heat is insidiously stretching its tentacles into the early morning hours. I grab my scarf from the floor, and wrap it around me, swinging my legs reluctantly off the bed.

She grunts and turns, farting softly in her sleep. The bile rises in my throat, my stomach heaves and I rush outside, retching quietly into a pretty flowerbed.

The early morning rays have lent the garden an ethereal glow. Dewdrops glisten on the leaves as I hastily nudge some soil onto my pale, watery vomit. The neighbour's dog barks, immediately setting off all the locality strays. Their chorus has a lone soprano whose unearthly howl is interrupted by the elderly *chowkidar*[1], who bangs his stick impatiently and shouts "BE QUIET!!!" Silence, then a howl as stick connects with backside... and the strays run helter skelter...

I breathe deeply. The air is fresher outside. The day's smog is yet to penetrate the atmosphere. I look down at my work roughened hands. They shake slightly. I take another breath and try to focus.

I walk back into the room and find her eyes concentrated on me. Grey, rheumy, needy. She indicates she requires help getting up. I turn away, pretending not to notice. I walk to the kitchen and start preparing the first of the many cups of *chai* [2]that will be demanded of me.

8am: The flowers and the sweets are arriving in a steady stream. I feel like a marionette, strings jerking me everywhere.

"Lajjo come here", "Lajjo put this away...not there, you silly girl...there!", "Lajjo, make me another cup of tea", "Lajjo, Lajjo, Lajjo" rings in my ears constantly.

"Yes *memsahib*[3]", I murmur dutifully, "Yes *sahib*[4]."

A courier whistles at me appreciatively. I have no time to even register his look. Sweat dampens my armpits, and I know I smell foul. This *salwar kameez* [5]hasn't been washed in a few days, and the synthetic fibres keep absorbing and retaining every odour they have ever come in contact with - from the lamb curry two nights ago, to the onion *bhajis*[6] I'm frying right now.

10am: The house guests are finally awake. They keep talking about something called jet lag. London is very far away they tell me. It took them nine hours to get here. I shrug. It takes me twice as long to get to my village. I still wake up at 5am to milk the cows.

Priya, their little one, barely six, comes and cuddles with me. I hug her back. Her eyes are still full of sleep, and her ponytail is askew. She reminds me of Rani, my sister. I miss her desperately, and Priya's affection is scant consolation at times.

Her sister walks in and eyes me warily. I cannot imagine what she has seen or guessed at, but she never lets her guard down. I overcompensate by hugging her with equal ferocity. She wriggles away.

"Mahi, are you hungry? Some biscuits with your milk? Would you like cornflakes?"

She nibbles at her toast, barely drinking her milk and turning away from the biscuits. The child is too thin. Why don't they feed her enough? At her age I could walk miles to fetch water. She is barely able to walk to the kitchen.

12noon: Everyone is finally awake. Last night's drinks have ebbed into this morning's hangovers. Coffees, teas, more coffees. The *Ayah* (Usha) from next door comes to give me a hand. She chats incessantly. My attention wanders, but I can't help but be riveted by stories of 'Baby', the seventeen year old wild child next door. She has a drug habit and an abortion that's been hushed up. The father is at his wits' end and the mother is seeking spiritual enlightenment in an Ashram. We smile conspiratorially. High society and low society often have similar problems. I can think of a few wild ones from my village too, as can Usha. We get on with our work.

I re enter my room and help the old woman up. She stares at me reproachfully. She has wet herself. The smell of urine and sweat make me gag. I shove her into the bathroom and quickly strip off the bedding. She sits there incontinent and incoherent. I bathe her rapidly, trying not to touch her paper thin flaccid skin.

She hums to herself while I comb her hair. I catch snatches of an old Hindi song. I'm finishing up when memsahib enters.

"Lajjo, is Mama ready?" The old woman beside me stiffens. *Memsahib* prattles on. "Oh good. All nice and fresh, Mama? Bring her out, will you? She can sit with the guests for a while."

The old woman's dislike for her daughter-in-law is legendary. She was the woman who stole her beloved son. But *sahib* never bothers with his mother. He barely even sees her, just as his father before him never did. *Memsahib*, for all her faults, makes sure the old lady is fed and taken care of. Not that she forgets to remind her husband of this fact every so often, ever so subtly.

2pm: I sweat over the *chapattis*.[7] The kitchen is like a furnace. There is no fan and when a bead of sweat falls into the potato curry, I just stir it in.

More guests have arrived and they are too busy regaling each other with stories to notice me. I keep replenishing their plates, and the London memsahib is the only one who thanks me.

Raj *bhai*[8] has just woken up, and he is tickling Priya who is giggling uncontrollably. I almost drop the dish I'm holding. Sahib's voice is like a whiplash, "You idiot! You nearly ruined our Persian carpet!"

The London *memsahib*, they call her Juju, takes it out of my hands and places it on the table. She is pretty and she is kind. I see how Raj *bhai* watches her when she is unaware. Her husband, pot bellied, with a pug like face, is too busy talking stocks and shares with his uncle, my *sahib*. He doesn't care enough to notice their little flirtation.

3:30pm: The last of the dirty dishes have been cleaned and put away. I've scarcely lain down and I hear a whisper. I open my eyes warily to see Juju *memsahib* smiling down at me apologetically.

"Lajjo, I hope you don't mind... I know it's an imposition... You've been so busy..."

Yes, yes... get on with it, I feel like saying, arranging my face into polite curiosity.

"Auntie wants me to go to the salon with her.... I really can't refuse... Would you keep an eye on the girls for me...?"

I nod and smile. Maybe there will be an extra 100 rupees in it for me, I think churlishly, while they spend 1000's getting prettified.

The children sit watching loud garish cartoons, while I doze fitfully. Priya lies next to me, smelling all flowery and fresh, my rancid smell covering her.

Mahi sits at a distance, watching the screen, and her sister in equal measures.

I dip in and out of strange, disconcerting dreams. My mother is in one of them. Not as I saw her last; laid out on the funeral pyre, dressed in her bright red wedding *saree*, the *bindi*[9] and the ash covering her entire forehead, as my father stood ready to light her up. No, she is younger: still well, still happy. Singing to me as she sews a button on my shirt. Then, just as suddenly, she's gone. To be replaced by the sharp tongued harpy my father married, who is now singing to *her* daughter,

9

as I wash the floor. I weave in and out of consciousness, feeling a hand on my thigh... and then not... I whimper, and then am completely awake. Priya is asleep and Mahi watches me with her measured gaze.

5PM: The marquee has been put up and the caterers are arriving. The air is heavy with the scent of marigolds. Sahib is directing the men to lay out the stalls in a particular order. *Memsahib* is talking to the wedding planner.

"Roshni, I want a good mix of music.... Bollywood, yes, but more western... Madonna, Rihanna... you know…"

The bemused wedding planner is nodding at the instructions.

There are lights everywhere, and the band that will escort Raj *bhai* on his mare are making themselves comfortable in the corner, with their refreshments. They'll need a lot of *samosas* [10] for stamina.

I feel a bit sick and sweaty, and the sudden trickle of blood between my legs doesn't help.

I catch Raj *bhai's* eye as he comes out of his room. He winks at me. I look away, and when I look back, he's gone.

The evening is a blur of activity. I iron shirts and *sarees* and dresses for the little girls. I coax the old woman into the living room where she sits like a grand old Buddha, belching lightly into the air. The men laugh, smoke and crack open bottles of whiskey. The women float about in their chiffons and their diamonds in a cloud of expensive perfumes.

I finally get to the bathroom, and turn on the tap to fill my bucket. I examine my naked body meanwhile. The breasts are beginning to sag. After all, I am not that young anymore. Twenty eight and I have spied my first grey hair. Not on my head but *there*. Nestling there so comfortably, as though it's always belonged. A sob catches in my throat. But I wash myself, scrubbing vigorously, till I have emptied my mind and heart.

The homemade pad sits awkwardly between my legs, chafing my thighs as I walk. I smell fresh though... a bit like the jasmine flowers I've put in my hair.

8:30pm: The pounding in my head seems to be in rhythm with the music outside. The wedding procession is almost ready to leave. The band is blaring out a brand new hit Bollywood number with great gusto... The extended family is dancing, drunk on the moment... this great joyous moment of the union of two families. And what a union it is! Two big players joining forces... Two major Industrialists coming together... What a merger! What a marriage!

Raj *bhai* looks very dapper in his *sherwani*[11] and turban. Juju *memsahib* is melting under his gaze. Her hand hovers a little too long on his lapel, and then with a laugh and a blush she moves on. He pulls the curtain of flowers down over his face. Someone helps him up on the mare. There is a lot of cheering and hooting. The wedding procession starts its slow march. Not far to go. After all, the bride lives just two streets away.

I watch them leave. No one notices me. Or so I think. Then I look around to see Mahi's eyes on me. There is curiosity and a smidgen of sympathy. But my answering gaze is savage, and alarmed, she runs to join her mother.

9pm: After all the frenzied activity of the last week, the sudden quiet is a welcome respite. I can still hear them in a distance... but it is fading...

They won't be back till later. Much later. And tomorrow, it'll start again. Might as well enjoy the peace.

The old woman sits in the room patiently, waiting to be fed. I mash the rice and potato curry, and feed her absently, watching the latest episode of my favourite soap opera. I like the family dramas. All the women are so beautiful and the men so handsome. I like the way the camera zooms back again and again to their faces as they say something dramatic. I don't particularly like the cat-eyed, cunning one. That's the trouble maker. She reminds me of my step mother. There, she's lying again... lying to save her skin... and get the heroine into trouble. I gasp at the cheek of it! I hear an answering gasp from the old lady. I turn to her, surprised at her interest.

She is turning blue. At first I don't understand. And then I do. I watch frozen, as she keels over, ever so slowly… just like they do in my soaps. There are grains of rice still stuck to the corners of her mouth. I wait for some kind of a dying declaration. But none comes. The air is heavy with her silence.

I look at her lying there; so fat, so old, so *dead,* and start to laugh. My shoulders shake helplessly, and I double up. My stomach hurts as I laugh and I laugh and I laugh.

I laugh till tears stream down my face.

SCORCHED

MUTHUSWAMY:

The sweat trickles down between the valley of her pubescent breasts like a little tributary feeling its pull towards a larger ocean. My eyes follow its progress greedily, till I feel her gaze upon me and hastily avert mine.

"Saras, get me a cool drink! I am about to die here."

My wife dutifully fetches me the drink, while I covertly watch her fourteen-year-old sister through half lidded eyes.

There is little respite from the heat on a May afternoon, and lying on the verandah in my rocking chair, I fan myself vigorously. The perspiration pools under my armpits, and a rancid odour rises up to meet my nostrils. The flies buzz in a soporific rhythm, lulled into a dull acquiescence. I swat the occasional mosquito away, pretending to doze, all the while scrutinising her.

She is not beautiful. She is dark and thin. Her lower lip protrudes, giving her sulky visage an ill-tempered hue. Yet, there is something so tempting, so very attractive about her. She is like a mango on the threshold of ripeness. Waiting to be plucked off the tree. Waiting for someone to bite into it, letting its sweet and sour juices run unfettered over the chin.

It has been a while since I felt this way. My wife arouses no ardour in me anymore. She is always busy around the child, fussing and spoiling and cajoling *ad nauseam*. I am so very bored of her, and of this tedium of married life. There has been no excitement in my life for a while now. I rise early, bathe, eat a breakfast of yogurt and rice, and head to the shop. I work hard, and profitably. I return home to tea and *pakora*[1], and a dinner of rice, *sambhar*[2] and *pappadum*[3]. She chatters to me incessantly about her day that is filled with inconsequential tasks. She gossips about the neighbourhood women. I half listen, and then turn in as quickly as I can.

Sometimes we make love, if I can be bothered, and if she isn't feigning a headache. It is a quick fumble and a half hearted attempt at intimacy. Occasionally, I get a glimpse of the loneliness in my soul, and hastily avert my gaze.

Pushpalata:

He is always watching me. Creepy old man. I have never liked him. Not when *Appa*[4] introduced him to the family. Not when *Amma*[5] approved of him as a potential suitor for her darling daughter. And definitely not when *Akka*[6], beautiful, intelligent, can-do-no-wrong *Akka*, decided that this would be the man who would keep her in comfort for the rest of her life. I barely attended the wedding then, truculently hiding up a tree, lured down only by the promise of hot *gulab jamans.* [7]

It's been five years since the grand wedding. She often comes to visit. More to show off her heavy *Kanjeevaram sarees*[8], and gold bangles that he buys her with monotonous regularity. They sit and chat in the front room, *Amma* and her, bonding over their love of all things shiny and new. I lurk in the background, as I always have.

Now, they have left me in her care. *Amma* and *Appa* off to Rameswaram on pilgrimage for a month. And here I am, sweltering in the month of May, in this capacious cavern of a house, with no trees to climb nor books to read.

There is the child though. He is so beautiful. Every time I look at him, my heart melts a little. He still has his baby curls, and a dimple on his left cheek. He smiles and holds up his arms to me, and is happiest when I carry him around on my hip, which is often. *Akka* has coolly designated me the child minder. Perhaps she can sense my love for him. She doesn't trust too many people with his care. I can spend hours with him playing peek-a-boo and listening to his delighted giggles. He sleeps with me in the afternoons, clutching at my blouse with one hand, sucking his thumb with the other. I run my fingers through his hair, smoothening the unruly curls, breathing in his warm baby smell.

Then I feel the eyes on me and shudder.

Saraswathi:

I cannot abide the girl. Sullen and ungrateful brat that she is. Never a smile on her face. It's almost as though she belongs to another family. *Amma* and *Appa* are so gracious. Such lovely, genteel people. I have always been compared to Appa's mother, a renowned beauty of her time. I have Amma's grace and fluidity.

Why, my *Bharatanatyam* [9]had been so faultless that my teacher was absolutely devastated that I did not take it up professionally! I had so many options ahead of me. Yet, I had known all along, that all I wanted in life was to be a homemaker. To take care of my husband and children. To have a house that was the envy of all my peers. I have all this, and more.

The girl, however, is a thorn in my side. Who can believe she is from the same gene pool? She has neither beauty nor grace. Not even good manners to hide her shortcomings. I have seen so many of my friends do a double take when I introduce her as my sister. So often I've joked that we picked her up from an orphanage.

It's only been a week of having her under the roof and already I feel irritated. My husband barely speaks to her, and when he does she responds in mono syllables. Ungrateful wretch! Can she not at least be polite to the man who's feeding and housing her?

The only consolation is that my baby likes her. He follows her around like a little lamb. It gives me some respite. Motherhood can be so challenging. Much as I love him, I need some time for myself too.

"Pushpa, come and get him, no? He needs his milk." She comes and scoops him up in her arms, and he giggles delightedly. I watch, slightly vexed by the scene.

Vaikaasi Visaakam[10] is but a few weeks away. I have so much to prepare. My friends and I will visit all the temples to pray for the celestial union of our Lord Murugan and his consort Valli. New *sarees* to buy. Perhaps a gold chain too? Ah, but this heat! The fans offer no succour. I barely move out of the periphery of the breeze and my blouse is soaked through. Perhaps I will join my husband on the verandah. After all, a Sunday afternoon in the companionship of one's beloved spouse is surely the recipe for a good marriage.

Pushpalata:

An odour of raw onions assails my nostrils before his rough, callused hand closes over my mouth.

"Shhhh!!!" He whispers urgently, while I struggle vainly, trying to gasp for breath. He is too heavy for me and his body pins me to the bed.

"Nothing to be scared of dear," he coaxes, "just a bit of loving…"

I try to bite upon his hand but he laughs and then wallops me with his other hand. I am stunned into immobility, and in no time he has pushed my legs apart, and is assaulting me in my private region. I whimper in pain, and his hand comes down on my mouth again. I shut my eyes to the depraved pleasure on his face.

It seems to carry on for an eternity. Then when he grunts and collapses on me, I know it is finally over. The child sleeps innocently unaware by my side, while the father lies spent atop me.

Suddenly he wakes up to his surroundings, and is off me like a bolt of lightening.

"Don't say a word," he cautions. "This… this is between us, alright? No one need know. No one will believe you anyway. So keep quiet, and all will be well…"

He waits for my nod before he creeps out of the room as quietly as he came in.

Waves of nausea wash upon me. I turn on my side and am sick

almost immediately. The baby awakes and starts to cry. I cry alongside.

Muthuswamy:

I feel scared and ashamed. She is only a child, and what I have done is tantamount to rape. I could be arrested for this. I could lose everything. How stupid could I be? Is it the heat that addled my senses?

Only, seeing her lying there, her skirt ridden up to her waist, abandoned to sleep, I could not resist myself. I replay it scene for scene in my mind, and cannot help but feel a delicious shiver of forbidden pleasure.

What if I am found out? Will she tell? I could deny everything. They would believe me, would they not? I wipe the sweat off my brow and think. I have to warn her... threaten her if I must.

I hear the wailing coming from her room and hurry before anyone else hears.

She is cleaning up her mess. The baby is sitting up on the bed, crying. He senses my eyes upon him and is momentarily quiet, before breaking into a fresh wail. She looks up slowly at me. There is a vacant blankness in her eyes, and in that instant I know I am safe.

Saraswathi:

I do believe the girl has developed a crush on my husband. She is always watching him. I have noticed how she shivers as he passes her. Oh, for goodness' sake! Does she really think he'll pay her the slightest bit of attention, ugly mangy thing that she is?

And all that moping around. As though the sky was about to cave in. I have tried asking her if she's missing *Amma* but she doesn't answer. Just stares into space, pretending as though I don't exist. I am really quite fed up with her. Another few weeks and I will be rid of her. *Cannot wait.*

Dearest husband though has been so very generous again. In fact, more than generous. The gold chain he has bought me must at least be 5 *tolahs*.[11] I cannot wait to display it on *pooja* [12]day. The wretched tailor is late making the blouse again. He says I have put on weight. What rubbish! He is merely trying to save the extra cloth for his collection. As though I do not know his thieving ways.

I try to cuddle the baby who pushes me away. He lisps the girl's name. I cannot believe it! Is she trying to supplant me in my child's affections too? I hug him to me forcibly, ignoring his yelp of discomfort. He smells of curdled milk. I call out to the girl to give him a bath. She might as well make herself useful.

Pushpalata:

I feel as though I am in the depths of a nightmare from which I cannot awaken. I feel so far removed from the minutiae of life. I carry on because I must. I have no recourse.

Akka is delegating extra work to me and it is a relief. I keep my hands busy and my mind emptied. I stay as far away from him as I can. His very presence terrifies me. But I watch him closely. I wedge the chair under the door handle every day and every night. He will not catch me unaware again. I sleep little and eat even less. I feel myself shrinking. I am trying to disappear, till I become so tiny. Like a little dot that no one will ever find.

The child knows I am not right. He follows me around even more. He tries to make me smile now, playing peek-a-boo with his little pudgy hands. He clings to me and tries to infuse my body with his baby warmth. I cannot respond.

Muthuswamy:

She has not said a word, and finally, I am able to relax. At first my nerves were on razor's edge. All at once the things I had taken for granted: my home, my family, the good name of my ancestors lay at the mercy of the girl's tongue. I could not believe how I had let a moment's ill judgement jeopardise all that was valuable and secure.

Slowly, however, I have allowed myself to breathe. I watch her surreptitiously though. She is like a puppet going through the motions, and a part of me feels sorry for her. The one time my gaze locked into hers, it was like peering into an abyss.

The strands of temptation start to coil around me unbidden. I cannot erase the memory of that snatched afternoon and yearn for more. My arousal grows as I watch her do the chores, bathe the child, and comb my wife's hair. Mundane tasks that have no eroticism to them per se, except for what her frail body imbues them with.

My mind starts to plan a dozen scenarios. I convince myself that she really wants me. Why else has she not spoken out?

I have tried the handle on her door a few times, but the little minx is keeping it shut somehow. How and where to corner her? I scratch myself languorously, wondering.

Saraswathi:

My *saree* weighs a ton and I find it difficult navigating through the masses of devotees in it. The sun is burning a hole in my back, and the jasmine flowers in my hair are limp and have lost their perfume along the way. My friends and I are being jostled along in the crowd and suddenly the oppressive heat, the myriad odours and the lack of air make me feel quite faint. I stumble and lose my footing in the throng. A few hands help me up. I feel one snaking around my neck, but before I can cry out, the chain is yanked forcibly off me. I scream. A few people look. Someone laughs, and everything goes black.

When I come to, I feel a glass of water at my lips. My friends mill around me, looking worried. I am sitting in a cool corner of the temple. I can hear the chants emanating from the main hall. I grope around my neck to startled exclamations from the insipid women around me. Of course it's not there! The thief saw his chance and took it. I lean my head back against the cold stone wall. Lata goes into hysterics.

"*Aiyyo Murugan*[13]*!!* What is the world coming to if a woman is not safe even in a place of worship? Such a beautiful chain that was! Oh Saras, what are you going to do?"

I collect myself, even as they calm her down. I need to go home. They want to accompany me, but I balk at that. I have to face the music alone. The thought of it makes me go quite pale, but I reassure them and hurry out.

The front door is shut, and I let myself in quietly. All I want to do is lay on my bed and sleep my worries away. I splash some water on my face, and then examine myself in the mirror. My face looks serene and composed as always, not revealing the turmoil inside. I hear what sounds like a laugh from the backyard and ignore it at first. Then curiosity overcomes me, and I head in its direction.

I wonder if my face is quite as composed as they both look up from their coupling to see me standing there. He looks shocked... and she, the little viper, looks at me blankly. The baby is watching them curiously. I shoot them both a savage look and turn on my heel in such anger that I nearly trip myself up again. A wild hot rage pulsates through me, and I turn around and spit out, "You... you little bitch! I want you out of my house now. NOW!" I scream and run inside, tears streaming down my face. He follows in pursuit.

Pushpalata:

"*Akka!*" I cry. I want to explain. I need to tell her the truth, but I fall silent as I remember the contempt in her eyes. I start to shiver.

The sun beats down mercilessly upon the small patch of grass and the few plants that surround it. My pitiful attempts to beautify the sorry patch remain just that. The shovel and the spade lay propped on the side, and the flower pot lies broken in the struggle that I had soon lost. The weeds are peering out from behind the uneven rocks that determine the border of the garden.

I listen but hear nothing. Nothing but for the occasional crow that ventures out in the afternoon. I start tidying the pot by setting it upright and scooping the mud back into it. My hands search for things to do while my ears reverberate with the finality of her words. I attack the weeds with a vicious ferocity. Yank. Pull. Set aside. Yank. Pull. Set aside.

The child waddles up to me. He tries to pluck at my skirt. I shoo him off. He retreats. He returns a moment later with his ball. "*Atthai!*[14] Atthai...*" He lisps.

He wants me to play. I shake my head and carry on weeding. He starts to cry, pulling and pulling at my skirt. I push him aside with as much force as I can muster. I hear his cry but ignore it. My ears are still ringing with Akka's words.

Suddenly I feel something warm and sticky under my feet, and notice belatedly that it is blood. The child lies motionless on his side, the ball still grasped loosely in one hand, a red pool spreading thickly under his head. I look up at the sky. A lone crow swoops down low, and then flies away.

I watch it leave till it is a mere speck in the sky.

MORALITY

IT WAS ANOTHER HOT, sticky day of July. The fan spun lazily above our heads, making no noticeable difference to the humidity. Summer was loath to give up its stranglehold over Delhi; while Monsoon hovered threateningly on the outskirts. So we perspired into our usual uniform of safari suits and waited patiently for the inevitable.

Our department wasn't that big. There was Bhambri, Kulbhushan, Lata, Jagannath (Jaggu) and I. Lata, being the only woman amongst us, would charm us into doing her share of the work, while she sipped her cups of *chai*,[1] and exclaimed over the love lives of the film stars in Stardust magazine.

We were a happy family of sorts. Each of our roles defined. Who would get the *samosas*[2] today? Who would order the *chai*? There was always enough gossip to occupy us. The other departments were larger and had a cross section of characters we loved dissecting.

Life had been smooth sailing till Narang had arrived. Tall, very thin and very young. His turban would sometimes sit askew on his head, undermining all the authority he wanted to project.

"*Arré yaar! Kahaan se aa jaate hai yeh kal ke chhokre!*[3] Teaching us our jobs, eh?" Bhambri said through his *paan*[4] stained mouth.

I laughed, of course. *Kal ka chhokra.* Born yesterday? Appropriate.

We were having our usual morning moan about Narang.

It had barely been a month since Narang had arrived as the Manager. He had made his intentions clear at the very outset. He was going to tighten the screws on this department. No more corruption. No more laziness. No more endless cups of *chai* and gossip. Oh no, Sirree! This was going to be a very tight ship indeed; with a very wet behind the ears Captain at the helm.

We'd sniggered into our cups. They all started out that way. New brooms and all. How soon it petered out depended on how much passive resistance we put up and the moral fibre of the individual in question.

"A month, tops," muttered Lata.

Well, that month was nearly over, and Narang showed no signs of backing off.

"Hitler has nothing on this guy!" said Jaggu. "Day after day, noses to the grindstone. He looks at each and every tender, man."

"Let him look," said Kulbhushan. "Physically impossible long term. *Kab tak karega[5]*? How long will it last? He'll have to start relying on us soon enough. Then the dry spell is over."

Yes, the dry spell was wreaking havoc on our finances. Our basic salaries had always been supplemented with the kickbacks that we received from our clients. What in our Delhi parlance was known as *"chai-paani[6]"*. It was custom. No one questioned it. Each time a tender was submitted, it came with a box of sweetmeats. Inside the box was an envelope stuffed with sufficient (or insufficient) Rupees 500 notes. Depending on the merits of the box, and the tender (but naturally), the contract would be awarded to the highest bidder. There were losers, of course. But, in my opinion, there were more winners.

Jaggu perched a tea cosy on his head, and adopting Narang's giraffe like gait, started pacing up and down the room. He frowned at us, and in a deep voice intoned,

"There is no place for corruption in this office. We are all paid a salary to do our jobs. We must do it honestly and to the best of our abilities…"

At this point, the tea cosy slipped off Jaggu's head, and we all fell about laughing.

I was the first one to catch his eye. I stood up hastily.

"Good Morning Sir."

"Good Morning," he said quietly. "I hope you are all having a very good one."

Lata blushed and started reorganising her files. Bhambri chewed on his paan thoughtfully. Only Jaggu, the halfwit, still stood grinning, tea cosy in hand.

"There is a very large tender coming in today. An Italian company. I'd like you to have a look at it."

He looked at me. "Once you've checked out the details, I want a report in my office. 4pm sharp."

He turned and left as silently as he had come in.

"Bloody Narang!" Jaggu exploded. "At least he could have the good grace to be a bit noisy. Your day is a write off, man. *Chal*[7], better get to work. Lataji, forget about the *samosas* and Sridevi. Get to work madam…"

Lata gave him a withering look and took out her nail varnish and planted it with a thwack on the table.

My day was spent poring over the fine print. The heat had dulled my senses and several times I had to go back and re read the previous page. My armpits were wet and my brow dripped sweat. I worked out the numbers in my head. I had always been good at numbers. Something didn't add up. I worked it out again. Then I looked for my underused calculator. It still didn't add up.

"Bhambri?" He looked up at me questioningly. "There's something amiss with this tender, *yaar*[8]. Figures aren't adding up. Will you have a look for me?"

He waddled over obligingly. Ten minutes later, he looked up, his eyes gleaming.

"What? What? Did you figure it out?"

He smiled and took out another *paan* from the little box he carried with him. Excruciatingly slowly, he placed it in his mouth. Then he grinned, revealing his blackened incisors.

"This is it, Chopra. This is our meal ticket."

He said it so softly, that at first, I nearly didn't catch it. It was obvious that he didn't want the other three to hear.

"Meal ticket? What do you mean?"

"Look at the names."

I did. Nobody I knew. There were a few Non Resident Indians in there and some Italians. Quattrochi, Gattuccio, Farfaglia. They all sounded like pasta to me anyway.

He wiggled his eyebrows at me. "This goes right to the top, Chopra. Right to the top. Narang doesn't know it yet, but the shit's going to hit the …" He looked up, contemplating the fan.

My mind darted around putting the facts together. He caught my startled look with a smug one of his own.

"And the figures?"

"Who cares about the figures? So they don't add up. *Arré*[9], we are small fry. The big kickbacks happen at the very top. What we get is chicken feed."

I knew this was true. But this time, could it be? After all, we were talking about the Prime Minister of the country. The same idealistic young man, who'd come into power on a tidal wave of sympathy after the assassination of his mother, the former PM. The one whose foreign wife had adopted India and its customs as her own.

Surely not.

But the figures told a different story.

"What should I do?"

"You must do your job. You must do it honestly, and to the best of your ability…" He deadpanned.

I sat there, file in hand, mind spinning through the permutations of consequences this could unleash.

Was Narang involved? I doubted it. He would hardly have handed a file of such importance to me so nonchalantly. If I took the facts to him as they were, he would have to take action. Either way, my responsibility ended there. He was my superior. Whatever happened next, it would be his head on the chopping block, not mine. Sometimes it was a comfort being at the bottom of the food chain.

Bhambri watched me with a sly smile on his face. "You've worked it out, my friend. Either Narang joins the club, or gets thrown out of it. Win win."

4PM ARRIVED TOO SOON for my liking. I shut the door to Narang's office and waited inside patiently.

The air conditioning whirred quietly in the background. Narang looked up from his desk coolly.

"Have a seat, Mr Chopra. You have looked over the figures?"

My forehead broke out in beads of sweat. I sat myself down reluctantly. The next half hour was spent explaining what I felt was so out of whack with this tender. Narang watched me steadily, his face betraying nothing.

When I had finished, he leaned forward, and gently took the file out of my hands. He flipped through it, pausing at several points. My palms were sweaty. I couldn't wait to get out of his office. To get home and ask Asha, my happy, pretty wife of two years, to get me a tall Johnnie Walker on ice. He finally placed the file on the desk and looked at me.

"What do you think we should do, Mr Chopra?"

I shook my head to clear it. This wasn't part of the script. I should have been absolved of all responsibility when I handed the file over. Why was he asking me? Wasn't he paid to make the decisions around here?

"Sir... I... I... really can't say."

"You know, Mr Chopra. I have always wondered about you. I didn't think you were like the others," he flicked his head distastefully. "You are the worker bee of the lot, aren't you? You've just had the misfortune to be lumped with them."

I sat there staring back at him. He looked at me contemplatively. "Keep this between the two of us. Leave it with me to handle."

I stood up gratefully. This was not the best moment to tell him that Bhambri already knew.

LIFE WAS routine for the next few weeks. The workload was heavy, and the rains, although threatening, never actually came. The air got muggier and our tempers got shorter.

Thud! The files landed on the floor. Jaggu stood up in a rage.

"*Saalé, Kutté*[10]! Bloody Dogs! Can't even provide an air conditioner for us. One bloody fan that is stuck at some prehistoric speed!!"

He attacked the regulator with an alarming ferocity.

"Jaggu! What are you doing?", screamed Lata. "You'll break it - and then we'll have no fan at all!"

Kulbhushan looked over at him and laughed. "You should have asked for vacation, Jaggu. I am going tomorrow to Nainital. Myself, the wife and our three children. Ahhh... cool mountain air. Boating on the Naini lake. Who wants to be stuck in a stuffy office?"

"Alright for some," muttered Jaggu, picking up the files off the floor.

Narang walked in and gestured to me. I could feel Bhambri's eyes on my back as I walked out.

The last few weeks hadn't been kind to Narang. Lines had sprung up on his previously unlined face. He looked weary, and some might have said, he looked afraid.

He didn't ask me to sit this time. Instead, he poured himself a cup of tea and then absently handed it to me. Toying with his pen, he scratched his nose and then cast around the room, as if he couldn't quite decide how to start this off.

"They've asked me to quash it."

I knew what he was talking about. Of course I did. I still pretended ignorance.

"Mr Chopra - that tender!" He twitched nervously. "Those figures... They've asked me... No, told me... to turn a blind eye. Suppress the file. Sort out the figures... that sort of thing..."

I looked at him measuredly. Almost wearily, he shook his head. "I can't do it."

"Why not sir?" In spite of myself, I had grown to like him.

"My conscience doesn't permit it, Mr Chopra. I have been brought up to believe in certain values. My family has followed the Gandhian ideology…" Here he smiled, catching my eye. "Yes, the irony doesn't escape me…"

"But sir, these are powerful people. People at the top. What could you possibly do?"

"I don't know. At this point, I honestly don't."

The air conditioner hummed contentedly. Jaggu would have had a wonderful day in this office, I noted pointlessly, to myself.

"What I am trying to say to you, Mr Chopra, is, that as far as those above me are concerned, only I came across the discrepancies. No one else was involved."

"Thank you, sir." I backed out of his office gratefully. This worker bee had work to do.

By Monday morning he was gone. His replacement was a dour old man named Chatterjee. Much to the relief of my colleagues, Chatterjee cared more about his home packed lunches than any work that did or didn't go on in the office.

Pleasant and humdrum. Life was simple again.

Narang's name never figured in the articles. But when The Indian Express and The Hindu blew the lid off the entire sordid B****s scandal, I knew who the whistleblower had been.

The fallout was long and hard. The Ruling Party lost the the public's faith, and the subsequent elections. The Prime Minister, image tarnished, desperately tried to prove his innocence. It was not to be. He was assassinated a couple of years later on his campaign trail. The case dragged on and on for two decades. The body count of winners and losers piled up. Was justice ever served? Who knows.

And who cares? Two generations down, B****s is a mere blot on India's inky history.

As for Narang, we never heard from him again. I often wondered how his principles were holding up in our brutal, relentless world.

Several years down the line, I did gather that Narang had migrated to America.

America? Ha! His incorruptible soul would do well there.

HEAVEN AND HELL

SHE PUSHED HIM HARD. He snapped back, "You are such a cry baby!" Sure enough, the tears were pooling in her eyes, her lip taking on a familiar quiver. Bindu stepped in quickly before the situation escalated.

"Stop it, you two! It's always the same with you. Either make up or go home. We're not here to watch you fight. We are here to play."

Sparrow twisted her face, and looked away. She knew her tantrum would have to wait. Avinash looked abashed. He was getting to the age where playing with girls would soon be uncool. He was still too young to join the older boys who played cricket on the *maidan*[1]. Our group of five girls had accommodated him from the very start. For one, he wasn't rough-and-tumble like the other boys. For another, we felt sorry for him. Poor, motherless boy.

It was only when Sparrow moved into the locality that the trouble had started. None of us really liked Sparrow. There was something very sly and shifty about her. Besides, she was permanently in a bad mood. But Mrs Kaul, Rupa's mum, had insisted we include her in all our games. Rupa was well liked in our group. Also, Sparrow's parents were their tenants. Consequently, Sparrow had become a little appendage to our crew. Barely tolerated, but there nevertheless.

I turned my attention to the game. Heaven and Hell. Heaven was any raised surface you could climb onto, before being caught. Hell was being caught, and put in the unfortunate position of the catcher. It was going well today. Arshi and I were the last ones left, and Rupa, between fits of giggles was trying to get a hold of one of us.

"Sonia, there there... Arshi, get on the wall quick."

The rest of them kept shouting instructions at us, till Rupa finally managed to grip the hem of my dress, and Arshi was declared the winner.

"Hello uncle," said Bindu, slightly startled. Sparrow's father had emerged quite suddenly behind her. His mad scientist look always made us uncomfortable.

"How is it going?" He boomed. Sparrow ran and clung to him. We smiled politely. "Come upstairs for a drink children. You must be worn out... all this running around in the heat..."

Since we had been playing on the street in front of their house, and intended to keep playing for a while, we had no choice. We followed him reluctantly.

Rupa whispered, "A quick *Rooh Afza*[2], and we'll leave. Promise."

We looked at her reproachfully. Baby, her sister, who was ever so slightly dim-witted, was the only one who grinned and nodded. Rupa could do no wrong in her eyes.

SPARROW and her parents lived in the rather cramped two rooms that had been let out to them by Rupa's parents. They weren't rich. Not even solidly middle class like the rest of our families. Yet, the way Sparrow's mum had furnished her living quarters, you would be at a loss to bracket them into any particular class or caste. Fab India[3] jostled with Khan Market [4]purchases. The curtains were some kind of gauzy fabric that billowed in the breeze, but couldn't possibly give them any protection from the merciless Delhi heat. There was an undone air to the entire place, something that discomfited us. Us with our Rexine sofas, striped curtains and Sarojini Market[5] bed covers. 'Bohemians' I had heard my mother mutter to my father sometime ago. I didn't know what that meant, but from the disapproving tone, I gathered it was something really bad.

To look at Sparrow's mother though, you couldn't imagine her being anything bad. She was just too beautiful. Even us, as children, were dumbstruck in her presence. She was rather dark and played up her complexion in vivid vegetable colour textiles. Her large eyes were kohl lined and heavy lidded. She wore backless *cholis*[6] and *sarees* slung so low on her waist to be positively indecent. (Rupa's mother's words, not mine). Her hair was long, thick and worn loose to her waist. She could have been an actress. She certainly had friends from the acting world who came to visit. What she was doing in our little suburban locality was a mystery, and the subject of much gossip amongst the plump, nondescript housewives that peopled our block.

Those doe-like eyes were focussed on me in puzzlement right now. Oh! Right. I had forgotten to answer her question. I nodded quickly, not sure what I was agreeing to, and was handed a ham sandwich with a glass of the crimson sweet concoction that I could tell had only been bought to appease Sparrow and her friends. Somehow, Sparrow's mum, or Mitali aunty as mother had asked me to address her as, didn't seem like a *Rooh Afza* sort of person.

When she turned her back, I quickly took the ham out of the sandwich and hid it in the potted plant. I was a Brahmin and couldn't eat meat, least of all pig meat. Rupa caught my eye and giggled.

"So, girls, have you played nicely today?" Mitali aunty probed gently. Her eyes fell on Avinash and she said apologetically, "and you, Avinash. I could hear you out there, laughing and running about. It must have been fun, na?"

"Yes aunty," chirped Baby. "We played *pitthu, oonch neech ka papda, kho kho*[7] and Heaven and Hell. So much fun. No school for another three weeks. So mummy allows us to play for longer. We have mostly done our holiday homework too."

She seemed to be laughing at us as she asked, "And what holiday homework did you get?"

An hour passed with us discussing our homework. Then Bindu decided to display the latest Kathak moves she had learnt at school.

We all danced to an Amitabh Bachchan [8]song, and finally Sparrow's dad brought out his guitar, and Mitali aunty sang a sad, sweet English song about love that none of us much understood.

"IT WAS NICE, *HAINA*[9]?" Arshi asked me as we walked back together.

"Yes, it was. I like Mitali aunty. She is so pretty and kind. Sparrow is so horrible. Do you think she's adopted?"

"No *yaar*[10]. Sparrow looks like uncle. She must be jealous because everyone likes her mummy and not her."

I digested this fact silently.

"Is that why she doesn't like Avinash either? We like him. He's a good boy and plays so well. He even has good ideas for new games. I'll miss him when he goes to the hostel."

Arshi blushed. She had been nursing an unrequited crush on Avinash for a while now.

"Oh sorry Arshu! I forgot. You'll miss him more, *na*[11]? Maybe he'll write to you? Or maybe he won't. Boys are not very good at writing letters. Anyway, let's make the most of these weeks before school starts. Then we'll only get to see him next year in the summer holidays."

A little deflated we returned home to our dinners and families.

HOW OR WHY we chose the street in front of my house the next day I'll never remember. But it all started out good-naturedly enough. Our usual games had been exhausted. We had broken up a fight between Sparrow and Baby. Mother had given us *samosas* with tomato ketchup, and we'd sat on the steps munching silently.

"My mother thinks you're stupid." Sparrow suddenly hissed to Avinash.

Avinash coloured slightly but decided to ignore her. He carried on licking the crumbs off his fingers.

"She thinks you have no manners and look like a girl." She persisted venomously.

"Sparrow…" Bindu warned, narrowing her eyes.

Sparrow ignored her. She had found her pace and nothing would distract her.

"Well, how could you have manners? You have no mother to teach you any. She ran away, didn't she? Didn't even take you with her. Na naa na nana." She stuck her tongue out.

Avinash's attack was so sudden and ferocious, that even nimble-footed Bindu couldn't react quick enough. He had managed to sock her one in the eye and tear a clump of hair off her head before we pulled them apart. They continued to struggle and scream, and Mother had to come downstairs to calm everyone down and dispatch all the children home.

"Sonia," Mother asked me later, "what is going on with all of you? You kids used to play so peacefully before."

I was too shaken to answer, refused all offers of *jalebi*[12] and milk, and went to bed instead.

NEITHER SPARROW nor Avinash came to our next few meetings. But Mother told me that the parents had met and brokered some kind of peace between the two. When we met next, they ignored one another but played nicely with the rest of us. An uneasy truce had been declared.

Mornings were spent at home, gathering up various flora and fauna for our Science project. Then after lunch and a nap, we were allowed out at 4pm, when the worst of the heat had dissipated. We then had a free run of all the streets in our block of the locality. Most people knew us and they put up with our noisy play with a sort of neighbourly tolerance. All except Mr Kalsi.

"Bloody children! Can't you bugger off and play somewhere else?"

He was an elderly widower of about seventy five with a grouchy temperament and a reputation for getting a little too familiar with his maids. He lived in one part of a rather decrepit bungalow. The other side had been left to rack and ruin. At some prehistoric time, someone had very optimistically nailed a TO LET sign on it. Over the years, one of the nails had come loose, and the sign hung askew. An 'i' had been inserted between the 'o' and the 'l', and just in case it wasn't clear enough, there was a rough sketch of a man squatting, with a large turd hanging off his bottom.

We were alternately attracted and repelled by the place. Attracted by all the possibilities of new games it offered us. Hide and Seek. Exploration of the Unknown and Scaring of the younger ones. Repelled by the aura of gloom that hung about it. The chance of it being infested by cockroaches and rats, or even a ghost or two. Mr Kalsi was purported to have been married to a very sickly woman who had died in the house. The more imaginative in our lot claimed to have seen a grey figure floating about at night, wailing and complaining of a tummy ache.

"Shall we go inside today?" asked Bindu.

Rupa hung back, holding on to Baby. I was game and so was Avinash. I could tell Arshi wasn't keen, but was willing to go along for his sake.

"No, you can't! My mother has said we can't enter other people's properties. It's called tres..tress… I don't know what it's called. But it is wrong!" Sparrow ended with a flourish. She delighted in pointing out the obvious.

Bindu sighed. Her attempts at livening up our games had failed again.

We dispersed soon after, promising to meet at the same time next day, this time at Avinash's house.

AVINASH WAS RICH. This much was certain. We knew it from the size of his house, from the décor and from the foreign car that stood on his drive. His father came from a very wealthy family, but had been disowned on account of having married outside their social strata. He had gone on to make his own millions, effectively thumbing his nose at his family. The fact that the marriage subsequently collapsed had not detracted from his aura. Mehra uncle was working from home today, and dismissed us to the garden after politely enquiring after our families and getting all the names muddled up.

Sparrow was unusually quiet. Out on the street, it was an equal platform. Here, in Avinash's house, she was at a disadvantage. She trailed behind us as we climbed trees and swung on the hammock. We ended up in Avinash's room, admiring the posters he had on his wall. Pop stars we had never heard of.

"Isn't this one from Wham?" Arshi asked shyly.

"Yes, and this one is Eurythmics… and this is Boy George." Avinash was enjoying himself. He rarely had an opportunity to show off. We were all rather impressed. Most of us had to share our rooms with our brothers or sisters. Like most Indian households, privacy was unheard of. Having one's own room, with a door with which you could shut out the outside world, was an enormous luxury.

"And who is this?" Sparrow asked softly.

We turned to her in surprise. Most of us had forgotten she was there. She was holding a sepia toned photograph of a woman with her face sightly turned away from the camera. The woman had a cigarette in her hand and she seemed to be laughing at something just outside the periphery. Avinash snatched the photo out of her hand.

"Where did you… how… how dare you…?" He spluttered, and suddenly, unaccountably, burst into tears.

We stood there, stunned.

Sparrow laughed. "You are such a ninny. Why don't you boast about this photo, huh? That's your mother, isn't it? The one who ran away. Maybe she didn't want to stay with a boy who behaves like a girl. You are such a girl. Why are you always hanging around us? Why can't you go and play with the other boys? Scared that they'll beat you up? 'Fraidy cat! Loser!"

"That's enough!" Bindu snapped. "Avinash has more guts than you.

He'll prove it too! Tomorrow, we'll meet outside Mr Kalsi's and we'll see who the 'fraidy cat is. Yes, that's right Sparrow, we are going inside the haunted house. You can wipe that smirk off your face because if you don't show up, you will be the loser. And you can forget about playing with us again!"

Arshi and I walked home, subdued and a little worried about the next day's challenge.

"I really don't like cockroaches, Sonia."

"I know. I'm not too fond of them myself. But it's Mr Kalsi that scares me the most. If he finds out, I am in BIG trouble. He's related to us."

"What? I didn't know this. How?"

For a while we discussed the complicated permutations of extended families. Then, worryingly, we came back to what was uppermost on our minds.

"That house has been empty for a long time. It must be really dusty inside." Arshi paused. "Do you think Sparrow will show up?"

"Well, if she wants to save face, she had better. But I kind of hope she doesn't. Then we'll be rid of her, *na*?"

"But Rupa's mum? She's always insisting we play with her. What if Rupa spills the beans?"

"Listen, Rupa won't say anything. And Sparrow daren't get on Bindu's wrong side."

"Yes, that's true... but..." She gnawed at her nail and came back to what bothered her most, "the house... what if there are rats?"

THE NEXT DAY was a Friday and our weekly visit to the temple. I prayed long and hard for a miracle, and was rewarded with a pat on my head and a *ladoo*[13]. I agonised over not going, knowing fully well I would.

"All but one," smiled Bindu. "Well, well, I wonder where Miss Sparrow could be?"

I caught Rupa's eye, and a nervous giggle escaped her. Bindu looked at her enquiringly.

"Only," she hastily supplied, "this morning we heard Sparrow's mother shouting at her father. Then she walked out. I don't know if she came back?"

We pondered this fact. Our mothers never shouted at our fathers. It just wasn't done. What a peculiar family. So, maybe Sparrow wouldn't show. That would let us off the hook. We sat on the wall and chatted for a bit.

"Of course, we could still go in," declared Bindu.

"Or not," muttered Avinash quietly. I looked at him, amused at his sudden reluctance.

"Well, it sort of defeats the purpose," he flared up. "I don't have anything to prove to you. It's that little fleabag that needs to be taught a lesson."

"Speaking of who…" Arshi interjected.

Sparrow was running towards us, all flushed.

Triumphantly, she came to a stop at the wall.

"I bet you thought I wasn't coming?" She said, her eyes gleaming. Since we couldn't deny this, we pretended to examine the bricks.

"What happened to your face?" asked Baby innocently.

"Nothing," said Sparrow, rather cross. "Well, are we or aren't we? Or are you just as chicken as him?"

At this, Bindu reasserted herself.

"Avinash, you get that rock from there to break the lock. It's so old, it'll probably just need a good whack. Sonia, Arshi, you come in behind me and be quiet. Sparrow, you go in first, since you seem so eager. Rupa," she turned to her kindly, "why don't you stay here with Baby and give us fair warning if anyone comes by?"

Rupa agreed readily but Sparrow was having none of it.

"Why can't Baby stay outside and Rupa come in? This is a quiet street and hardly anyone passes by at this hour. Why do we need two guards?"

No one could refute this logic, and Rupa reluctantly had to join our breaking-and-entering mob.

We had never been quieter in our lives. Partly due to apprehension, partly because we knew there was no turning back.

The house just stood there, like an entity in its own right. Grim and forbidding. The 'toilet' sign swung slightly in the breeze. Cobwebs had wrapped themselves many times over it, giving it a silvery sheen. The sky had darkened in the past hour, and there seemed to be a dust storm brewing in the distance. Little flurries of dust danced like whirling dervishes on the open porch. Arshi grasped my hand tightly. I gave it a reassuring squeeze, although I could not swallow the lump of fear in my throat. I looked over at Sparrow who seemed to have a look of desperate determination plastered on her face. Avinash was concentrating on not dropping the rock he held. Bindu led the way, fearless as always.

The lock didn't need any whacking after all. It had lost its battle against the elements a long time ago, and lay on the floor rather forlorn and useless. Bindu pushed the door, and it swung open noiselessly. We entered single file, bemused at how easy it had been. The interiors were gloomy, but not especially scary. Furniture had been covered with sheets that were further covered with dust. A black and white picture of a young Mr Kalsi and his pretty wife sat on the mantelpiece. We looked around at the unremarkable room, and conveyed our disappointment to each other with our eyes. Bindu motioned for us to explore further. Something scurried over Arshi's foot, and she jumped clapping her hand over her mouth to stifle a scream. Rupa turned white and clutched Sparrow, who shook her off with annoyance.

We shuffled in behind Bindu. It was all the same. Dull, dreary furniture, a few pictures on the walls, and a general air of neglect that hung in the air. Reality compared very unfavourably to the visions we had conjured up in our minds.

Outside, the dust storm had arrived, and where previously, we would've been ensconced in our respective houses, we were now stuck here, waiting for it to pass. Rupa was starting to worry about Baby.

When we heard the sob, we thought it was Rupa. But Rupa looked back wide eyed and shook her head. Arshi whispered, "It came from over there," indicating a door further down the hallway. A chill went down my spine and I wondered if Mrs Kalsi's ghost was about to declare herself. Sparrow looked at Bindu and then at Avinash. With her finger, she pointed to the door, as if to say, "Come on!" Avinash looked terrified. Bindu was slowly turning the colour of puce. Sparrow, with a vicious tenacity, grabbed Avinash's hand and started to drag him towards the door. Bindu stood powerless and rooted to the floor.

There was a clap of thunder and with a torrential downpour, the skies opened. We huddled close to one another. They were nearly there, and Sparrow, in her moment of vengeance had completely forgotten her fear. She grabbed the handle of the door and was yanked in as it swung open dramatically at exactly the same moment.

"Aiieeeeeee!" Rupa screamed and passed out. Bindu and Arshi ran outside in a panic. I stood there trembling, watching Avinash at first turn white, and then a deep, blotchy red. Abruptly, he turned on his foot and stomped out, a look of fury on his face.

Slowly, I made my way to the open door.

Sparrow stood there open-mouthed looking from her mother to Avinash's dad and back again. Mitali aunty's *saree* was abandoned on the floor, and Mehra uncle sat bare chested on the bed, smoking a cigarette. They all turned to look at me. Mitali aunty smiled absently, and picked her *saree* off the floor. I backed away as quietly as I had come in.

15 YEARS later

"Arshu, do you remember that Summer we discovered Mitali aunty's affair?" I asked Arshi over our monthly cappuccino catch-up.

"Hmmm… vaguely… It was all quite scandalous, *na*? So many years ago now."

"Funny, how Sparrow and Avinash never really fought after that…"

"Well, she wasn't really around for much longer. Didn't they move away?"

"Yes… and then a few years later Bindu eloped with that rather unsavoury character. Gosh, we did have some exciting times there!"

"I wonder what happened to Sparrow and the rest of them? Rupa emails me occasionally. She's just had a baby boy."

"Baby's still living at home. But here's the surprise! Guess whose article I came across in the newspaper today? Kruttika Ghosh aka Sparrow! She's made quite a name for herself."

Arshi skimmed the article with a smile on her face.

"Bitchy as always, I see?"

We laughed.

"She's putting her bile to good use."

"And Avinash?" She asked me rather wistfully.

I shrugged and turned to the sink to rinse out our cups. I knew he'd moved to New York with his male partner. But I didn't tell Arshi that.

Some illusions are best not shattered.

HIJRA

(eunuch)

The heat is appalling. The midday sun beats down mercilessly upon our bare heads. The tarred road seems to undulate under my feet, and I feel as though wave upon wave of hot air, incensed with cow dung and dog piss is reaching up to my nostrils. I trip over the hem of my *saree*[1]. Lata grips my elbow, steadying me, patting me in reassurance.

Sita cackles, "Whore! Can't you watch where you are going?" She is particularly waspish today. Disappointed that her tryst last night didn't go well. I ignore her and huddle closer to Lata.

Our motley crew makes its noisy way forward. There is a lot of discordant singing. We clap our hands together, as only we can. Brazen, defying all social taboos. We are the hijras.

I don't remember when I first realised I was different. I grew up in this community of strange half men/ half women. I knew no better. Lata was the mother I never had. Tender in her surrogacy and fierce in her protection. She was the one who taught me how to wrap a *saree* around my angular body, how to shave closely so that the 5 o'clock shadow wouldn't show up too soon. How also to apply the makeup with such precision that my masculine features would soften and blend into an accepted caricature of a woman.

"Move it girls. Move it! Not far to go now. It is on this street," Radha urges us on. She is the guru. Our leader of sorts. The one who keeps us together. Binds us in our misfortune.

Sita stops in protest. She uses the edge of her *saree pallu*[2] to wipe the sweat off her face. Sighing dramatically, she looks heavenwards and declares, "I cannot move another step, I tell you! This heat is destroying me. Look, all my makeup is washing off. Radha *ji* [3]are you sure we are going the right way? Only, the last few times, you have led us astray."

Her cronies giggle. Radha frowns at her. She knows where this is going. Her leadership has been in question for a while. Radha is ageing and sometimes her memory fails her. Sita has been biding her time. I shudder to think how things will change, as and when she does usurp the top slot.

We follow Radha, and Sita and her band join us again after some discussion. A hawker stares at us open-mouthed. He is but a boy. Sita winks at him lasciviously. An old woman we encounter crosses the street hurriedly, spitting in our direction, mouthing prayers. Ultimately, we come to a corner shop. I lean against the *peepal*[4] tree and fan myself while the others drink the Fanta offered by the shop keeper. He is a garrulous sort.

"Yes, yes. They had the baby on Friday. What is today? Hmmm, Monday. Yes, the girl has come to stay with the mother. She will stay at least two months. Husband hasn't come with her. What? Yes, it's a boy. Happy day for the family. After three girls, they finally get a boy."

More probing and he chats on happily.

"Business family... Jains you know. But there was some talk of the husband leaving her if she didn't have a boy this time. Yes, yes. Very happy. They distributed sweetmeats to everyone in the colony."

Radha offers him money for the drinks, but he refuses to take it. He wants our blessings. I cringe as we go through an elaborate display of blessing his shop, and he, in turn, touches our feet with such humility. To him, we are the *ardhanaris*[5], an amalgamation of Lord Shiva and Goddess Parvati. We are divine, and therefore able to confer blessings.

It is nearer 2pm when we arrive at the house. My feet feel swollen in my slippers and the shiny straps chafe on the blisters that have sprung up under them. The gates are locked and there appears to be no sign of life. We are used to this. Someone must have tipped them off. Radha clangs the gates and motions to us. Immediately we start our raucous singing. Some of us start to dance, swaying our hips in a strange parody of a Bollywood number. We sing a medley of songs. At first they are happy songs, but slowly they turn acerbic. Our singing is louder now and harsher. The curtains twitch.

An old woman comes out, head bowed and palms joined together. Politely she asks us to leave. Sita cusses her out.

"Ayah? They send an ayah?? Who the bloody hell do you think we are? Fucking bastards!"

Radha interjects, and calmly directs the woman to tell her memsahib that we won't leave till we have seen and blessed the baby. The old lady shuffles back inside.

We are in!

The new mother sits with the infant at her breast, looking scared and swollen. Her mother hovers nearby, offering us water and *ladoos*[6]. We want neither. Radha politely asks to see the baby, and the mother reluctantly hands her son over. Gently, his clothing is removed, and his genitals checked. My heart palpitates over this process, and a lonely lament leaves my lips unbidden. They sit dumbstruck as my song weaves its magical spell on my audience. I sing with my heart, and rarely are the recipients unmoved.

With a nod and a smile, Radha returns the child to his mother. All is well. The mother smiles shyly at me, and I give her head a little pat. Something wrenches in me as I belatedly realise that perhaps my mother was not quite as lucky.

We are offered Rupees 2000.

"Too little!" spits out Sita.

Radha bargains with a practised air. It goes on a while. I watch the baby suckling at his mother's breast.

We leave, happy to settle somewhere between the amount offered, and the amount demanded. It has been a good days' work.

WE DRESS in our finest for the wedding in the evening. Gaudy *sarees* and jangly bangles compete for attention with the lurid lipsticks and the jasmine flowers in our hair. In twilight, we are nearly attractive. It is no wonder that so many husbands come to find solace in our arms. We cannot offer them domesticity, but we can offer oblivion. If only for a few hours.

The *shamiana*[7] is decorated with a myriad coloured lights that twinkle from a distance. The cacophonous band blares an assortment of Hindi songs. It drowns out our approach.

Suddenly we are in the midst of the wedding guests. We are thrusting our pelvises and grinding against the men. It is our usual modus operandi. They move away from us in disgust. The women mutter and glance our way, riveted nonetheless.

We proceed towards the podium on which the bride and groom are being felicitated. There has been no offer of money yet from the stunned hosts. So we must continue to embarrass them till we are dispatched with a suitable payment. Sita is now threatening to disrobe and we lustily egg her on. Quite suddenly, she stops. Her eyes are on the groom, who has moved the flowers away from his face to view the kerfuffle. It is her paramour no less! With a renewed cockiness, she resumes her gyrations. I watch her closely. There is a brittleness to her.

The *lathi*[8] charge comes so suddenly that for a moment it seems to be a frozen tableaux. The groom's uncle is a sub inspector, and his police reinforcements aren't far behind. We are shoved out of the marquee to the sound of cheers. Outside, we are beaten to a pulp. Sita's *saree* is torn off her.

"You wanted to get naked? Come, let me help you," the policeman jibes. She clings to the tatters of her vestments, shaking in terror. Radha tries to intervene, and the heavy stick comes down on her head with a loud thwack. She is left to bleed on the side of the road, while we are taunted and groped and hit mercilessly, all in the name of law and order. Not a single passer by comes to our aid. The wedding party continues inside with an added frisson to its gaiety.

It is a broken and humbled crew that reassembles and limps our way back. We lean on each other : Radha on Sita, Lata on me. The tears come later. Much much later, when we are in our respective beds, cocooned in our loneliness and pain. We soothe ourselves to sleep. We have an early start the next day. We have work to do. We have money to earn.

With this thought, I drift off to sleep. To the land of dreams. The only landscape that affords no judgement.

Sign up today to hear of Poornima's new releases and promotions!

AFTERWORD

Word-of-mouth is crucial for any author to succeed. If you enjoyed the book, *please* do leave a review on your favourite site! Even if it's just a sentence or two. It would make all the difference by helping other readers to find the book, and would be very much appreciated by this humble author. :)

DO sign up to hear more about my new releases and any special offers plus get yourself a FREE story as a thank you!

Visit www.poornimamanco.com to keep abreast of all my news.

GLOSSARY OF TERMS

1. PARVATHY'S WELL

1. Mother
2. Father
3. A thin, very spicy southern Indian soup served alone or combined with other foods, such as rice, as a side dish.
4. Term of endearment
5. Fried vegetable frittatas
6. Term of endearment
7. A garment consisting of a length of cotton or silk elaborately draped around the body

2. LAJJO

1. watchman
2. Tea
3. Madam, respectfully
4. Sir, respectfully
5. Indian loose top and trousers
6. Onion frittatas
7. Indian flatbread
8. Brother, generic usage
9. Dot worn between the eyebrows, normally signifying a married woman, but used decoratively now.
10. Potato filled savoury snacks
11. A knee-length coat buttoning to the neck.

3. SCORCHED

1. Fried vegetable frittatas
2. South Indian lentil curry
3. A thin, crisp bread or wafer of India, made of lentil flour and usually flavoured with pepper and other spices.
4. Father
5. Mother
6. Elder sister
7. Indian sweet

8. Silk sarges from Kanjeevaram area in the South of India
9. Indian classical dance
10. South Indian festival
11. Measure of weight
12. worship
13. Oh God!
14. Aunty

4. MORALITY

1. Tea
2. Potato filled short crust pastries, normally deep fried. A savoury Indian snack.
3. Eh, chaps! Dunno where these newbies come from!
4. Betel leaves prepared and used as a stimulant.
5. How long will he do it for?
6. Euphemistic terminology denoting bribes
7. Come on
8. A casual way of saying friend
9. Hey
10. Asses! Dogs!

5. HEAVEN AND HELL

1. Field
2. Sweet squash drink
3. An Indian store that caters predominantly to a foreign clientele
4. A more upmarket area catering to the Delhi elite
5. Shopping area for the predominantly middle class clientele
6. Blouses
7. Indian street games
8. A very famous Indian actor
9. Right?
10. Pal
11. No?
12. Indian sweet
13. Indian sweet

6. HIJRA

1. Indian outfit
2. Long end of the sari worn over the shoulder
3. Term denoting respect
4. Fig/Mulberry tree
5. Half male, half female
6. Indian sweets

7. Marquee
8. Heavy, wooden stick

ALSO BY POORNIMA MANCO

Damage & other stories

Holi Moly! & other stories

The Intimacy of Loss

Twelve - stories from around the world

Parvathy's Well & Other Stories: The India Collection

A Quiet Dissonance

ABOUT THE AUTHOR

More about Poornima Manco

A bookworm since childhood, her imagination was channelled into writing by her mother. She won several competitions at School and University for her writing but never pursued it seriously. After several years of a writing hiatus, akin to being in writing Siberia, a competition in a newspaper reignited her love. The outcome was Parvathy's Well.

That story remains special as it once again set her on the path to writing, and reacquainting herself with her dormant creative self.

She lives and works in the United Kingdom, is married and has two teenage daughters.

You can follow her thoughts and musings at:
www.poornimamanco.com

Printed in Great Britain
by Amazon